A Note to Parents and Teachers

Kids can imagine, kids can laugh and kids can learn to read with this exciting new series of first readers. Each book in the Kids Can Read series has been especially written, illustrated and designed for beginning readers. Humorous, easy-to-read stories, appealing characters, and engaging illustrations make for books that kids will want to read over and over again.

To make selecting a book easy for kids, parents and teachers, the Kids Can Read series offers three levels based on different reading abilities:

Level 1: Kids Can Start to Read

Short stories, simple sentences, easy vocabulary, lots of repetition and visual clues for kids just beginning to read.

Level 2: Kids Can Read with Help

Longer stories, varied sentences, increased vocabulary, some repetition and visual clues for kids who have some reading skills, but may need a little help.

Level 3: Kids Can Read Alone

Longer, more complex stories and sentences, more challenging vocabulary, language play, minimal repetition and visual clues for kids who are reading by themselves.

With the Kids Can Read series, kids can enter a new and exciting world of reading!

Franklin the Detective

From an episode of the animated TV series *Franklin*,
produced by Nelvana Limited, Neurones France s.a.r.l. and
Neurones Luxembourg S.A., based on the Franklin books
by Paulette Bourgeois and Brenda Clark.

Story written by Sharon Jennings.

Illustrated by Céleste Gagnon, Sean Jeffrey, Sasha McIntyre, Shelley
Southern and Laura Vegys.

Based on the TV episode *Franklin the Detective*, written by Brian Lasenby.

 ™ Kids Can Read is a trademark of Kids Can Press Ltd.

Franklin is a trademark of Kids Can Press Ltd.
The character of Franklin was created by Paulette Bourgeois and Brenda Clark.
Text © 2004 Contextx Inc.
Illustrations © 2004 Brenda Clark Illustrator Inc.

Kids Can Press acknowledges the financial support of the Government of Ontario, through
the Ontario Media Development Corporation's Ontario Book Initiative; the Ontario Arts Council;
the Canada Council for the Arts; and the Government of Canada, through the BPIDP, for our
publishing activity.

Published in Canada by
Kids Can Press Ltd.
29 Birch Avenue
Toronto, ON M4V 1E2

Published in the U.S. by
Kids Can Press Ltd.
2250 Military Road
Tonawanda, NY 14150

www.kidscanpress.com

Series editor: Tara Walker
Edited by Yvette Ghione
Designed by Céleste Gagnon

Printed in China by WKT Company Limited

The hardcover edition of this book is smyth sewn casebound.
The paperback edition of this book is limp sewn with a drawn-on cover.

CM 04 0 9 8 7 6 5 4 3 2 1
CM PA 04 0 9 8 7 6 5 4 3 2 1

National Library of Canada Cataloguing in Publication Data

Jennings, Sharon
     Franklin the detective / Sharon Jennings ; illustrated by
Céleste Gagnon ... [et al.].

(Kids Can read)
The character Franklin was created by Paulette Bourgeois and
     Brenda Clark.
ISBN 1-55337-497-5 (bound).   ISBN 1-55337-498-3 (pbk.)

I. Gagnon, Céleste II. Bourgeois, Paulette III. Clark,
Brenda IV. Title. V. Series: Kids Can read (Toronto, Ont.)

PS8569.E563F71925 2004   jC813'.54   C2004-901107-3

Kids Can Press is a *l'orus*™ Entertainment company

Franklin the Detective

Kids Can Press

Franklin can tie his shoes.

Franklin can count by twos.

And Franklin can follow clues.

Franklin is a detective.

When he puts on his detective hat

and his detective coat,

Franklin is on the case!

One day, Franklin's mother went shopping.

She got home and put away the food.

Then she said, "I can't find my purse."

"I will find it," said Franklin.

"I am a detective."

He put on his detective hat

and his detective coat.

Franklin was on the case!

Franklin looked

in the car.

He looked

on the ground.

He looked all around

the kitchen.

Then he thought

for a minute.

"AHA!" shouted Franklin.

He opened the fridge.

The purse was beside the milk.

"Thank you," said his mother.

"You are a good detective."

The next day, Franklin saw

Beaver, Bear and Fox.

They had a baseball bat

and baseball gloves.

They did not look happy.

"AHA!" shouted Franklin.

"I have a hunch

that something is wrong."

"Yes," began Beaver. "We —"

"Wait!" cried Franklin.

"Let me guess!"

Franklin looked at his friends.

"Hmmm," he said. "You have everything for a baseball game except a baseball."

"You're getting warm,"

said Beaver.

"AHA!" shouted Franklin.
"You can't play baseball
because someone *forgot*
to bring the baseball."

Bear shook his head.

"We *had* a baseball," said Beaver.

"But Fox hit it into the woods."

Franklin jumped up.

"I'm a detective," he said.

"I will find your baseball."

"How?" asked Beaver.

"I will look for clues,"

said Franklin.

"Ooooooh," said everyone.

Everyone walked to the park.

"I stood here and hit the ball," said Fox.

"I saw it hit that tree," said Bear.

"We didn't see it again," said Beaver.

Franklin walked over to the tree.

He pointed to footprints on the ground.

"These are Goose's footprints," he said.

"You did not tell me

that Goose was with you."

"She wasn't," said Beaver.

"AHA!" shouted Franklin.

"I have a hunch that Goose

found your baseball!"

Everyone ran to find Goose.

"Did you find their baseball?"

asked Franklin.

"No," said Goose.

"But you were at the tree," said Franklin.

Goose nodded.

"I heard a thunk.

Then I heard a splash.

But I did not see

a baseball," she said.

"A splash?" asked Franklin.

"Hmmm."

He thought for a minute.

"AHA!" shouted Franklin.

"Follow me!"

Everyone followed Franklin to the pond.

"I have solved the case

of the missing baseball," he said.

"First, the baseball hit the tree.

Then it fell into the pond."

"Wow!" said Bear.

"You *are* a good

detective."

Everyone jumped into the pond.

But they did not find the baseball.

"Hmph!" said Beaver.

"You are *not* a good detective."

Everyone left Franklin and went home.

Franklin walked back to the park.

"I will follow the trail of clues

one more time," he said.

Franklin stood where Fox had stood.

He pretended to hit a baseball.

Then he ran over to the tree.

He threw a stone at the tree.

Thunk!

Splash!

An apple fell into the pond.

"AHA!" shouted Franklin.

"The baseball did not fall into the pond!

An *apple* fell into the pond!"

Franklin thought some more.

"But that means ..."

Then he looked up, up, up.

"AHA!" he shouted again.

Franklin picked up more stones.

He threw them at the tree

again and again and again.

Thunk!

Splash!

Thunk!

Splash!

Thunk!

Splash!

And each time, an apple fell
into the pond.

Franklin threw a stone at the tree

one more time.

He threw the stone

as hard as he could.

Thunk!

Bonk!

The baseball hit Franklin on the head.

"OUCH!" said Franklin.

Franklin ran to find his friends.

He gave Beaver the baseball.

"Yippee!" said Beaver.

"Where did you find our baseball?"

"It was stuck up in the tree,"

said Franklin.

"Wow!" said Bear.

"How did you get it down?"

"I'll give you a clue,"

said Franklin.

Franklin smiled.

"A good detective uses his head."